MW00956087

Sol & Luna

A Story of Two Friends, Gratitude, Love for Yourself, and Love for Others

Pearly Hidron

Copyright © 2019 Pearly Hidron

All rights reserved. The book author retains sole copyright to her contributions to this book. This book or any portion thereof may not be reproduced or used in any manner whatsoever without the express written permission of the author except for the use of brief quotations in a book review.

connectwithpearly@gmail.com

ISBN: 9781707708086

DEDICATION

To my loved ones, who encouraged and believed in me to contribute and create with one of my gifts to the world.

To you, magnificent being. Thank you for choosing this book. Your love and support means the world to me. I created this book for your enjoyment and I hope it earns a special place in your heart.

CHAPTER 1: TWO FRIENDS MEET

One rainy and cold evening, there was a dog named Sol, sitting on his owner's bed by the window.

Sol's belly was grumbling and he was already thinking about dinner.

As he was thinking of all the delicious food to eat, like biscuits and kibble, he noticed a small kitten hiding under a tree in the pouring rain.

Sol thought the kitten should come inside the house for warmth and dryness.

Sol went to find his owner first for permission to let the kitten in.

He nudged his owner to look out the window.

When the owner noticed the small wet kitten under the tree, she quickly went out in the rain to carry the kitten inside.

The owner wrapped a towel around the kitten to dry.

The kitten turned to Sol and let out a small meow,

"Hi I'm Luna, thank you for letting me in to stay warm and dry. I'm very grateful."

Sol displayed a wide smile,

"You're welcome Luna, my name is Sol and I'm happy my owner and I could take you in and offer you some warmth."

Sol paused and did not understand what *'grateful'* meant, it was a new word for him.

Sol asked,

"What does 'grateful' mean?"

Luna smiled and replied,

"Grateful means being thankful, showing appreciation for and returning to kindness."

Luna then softly closed her eyes, letting out a deep gentle breath and said,

"Just like how thankful I am to now have a roof over my head, this towel to dry me off, and a new friend."

Sol understood, wagged his tail in happiness, and hugged his new friend.

"I am grateful you are here too. Come with me, it's almost dinner time."

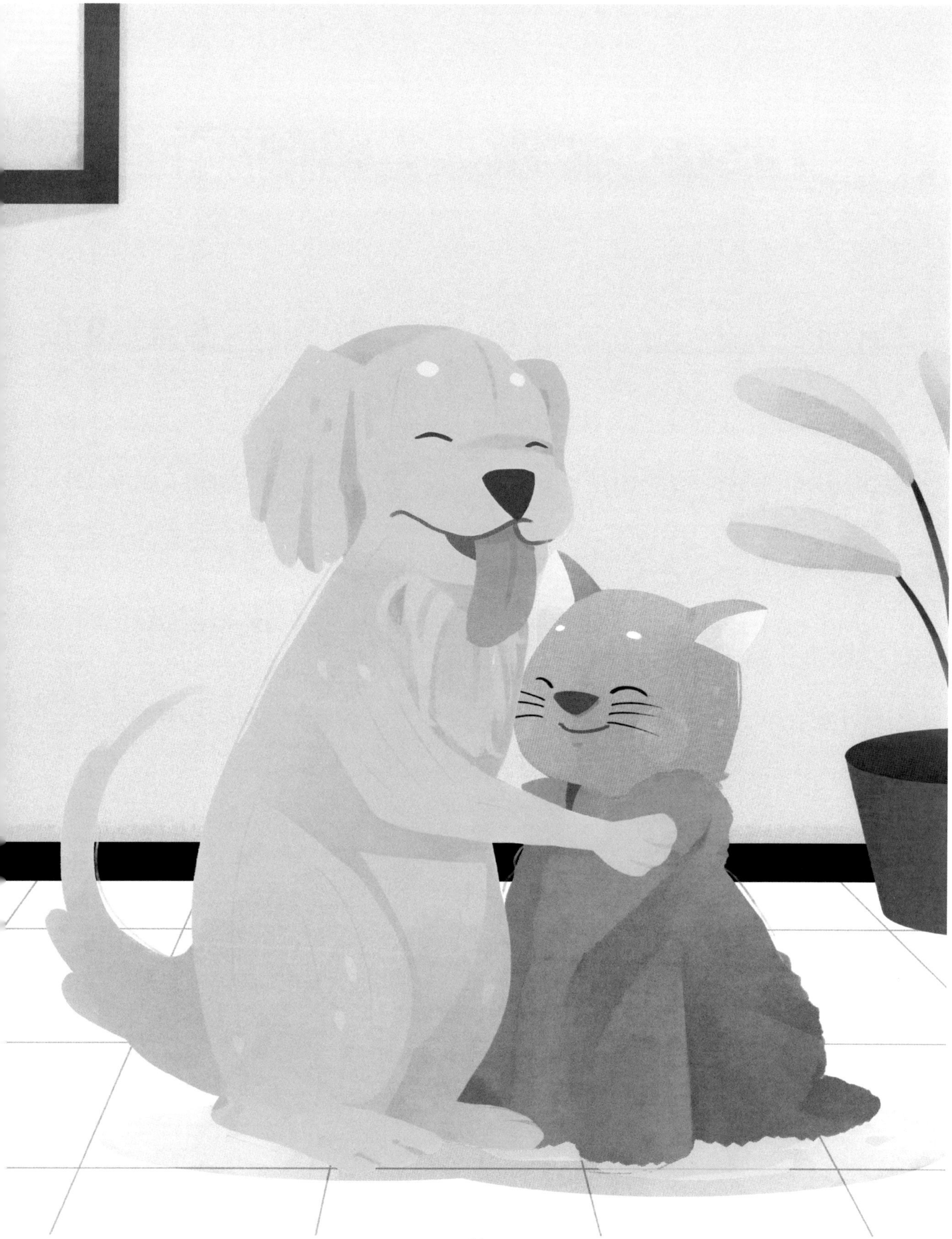

CHAPTER 2: STAYING IN THE PRESENT IS A GIFT

Sol excitedly ran ahead of Luna into the kitchen, almost forgetting she was trailing behind.

He saw the bag of kibble and biscuits by the shelf.

His favorite beef kibble and bacon biscuits, what a delight!

Sol's owner was already cooking in the kitchen and turned to Luna who was sitting patiently,

"I was planning on making salmon for dinner tonight, and will prepare some for you as well. I hope you like salmon."

Luna meowed with soft glee and the owner smiled.

She stroked Luna and said,

"You are the calmest kitty I have ever encountered."

A plate of beef kibble was placed in front of Sol and a plate of salmon for Luna.

Sol dove headfirst and ravenously ate his kibble.

Luna took one small bite, chewed slowly, and savored every bit of the salmon.

As Sol was close to finished with his kibble, he kept thinking about the next thing to eat.

He stopped midway and asked Luna what he should eat next.

Luna paused and replied,

"I already have this delicious meal and I'm currently focused on this salmon I'm eating. I do not worry what food I should eat next, it makes meal time so much more enjoyable."

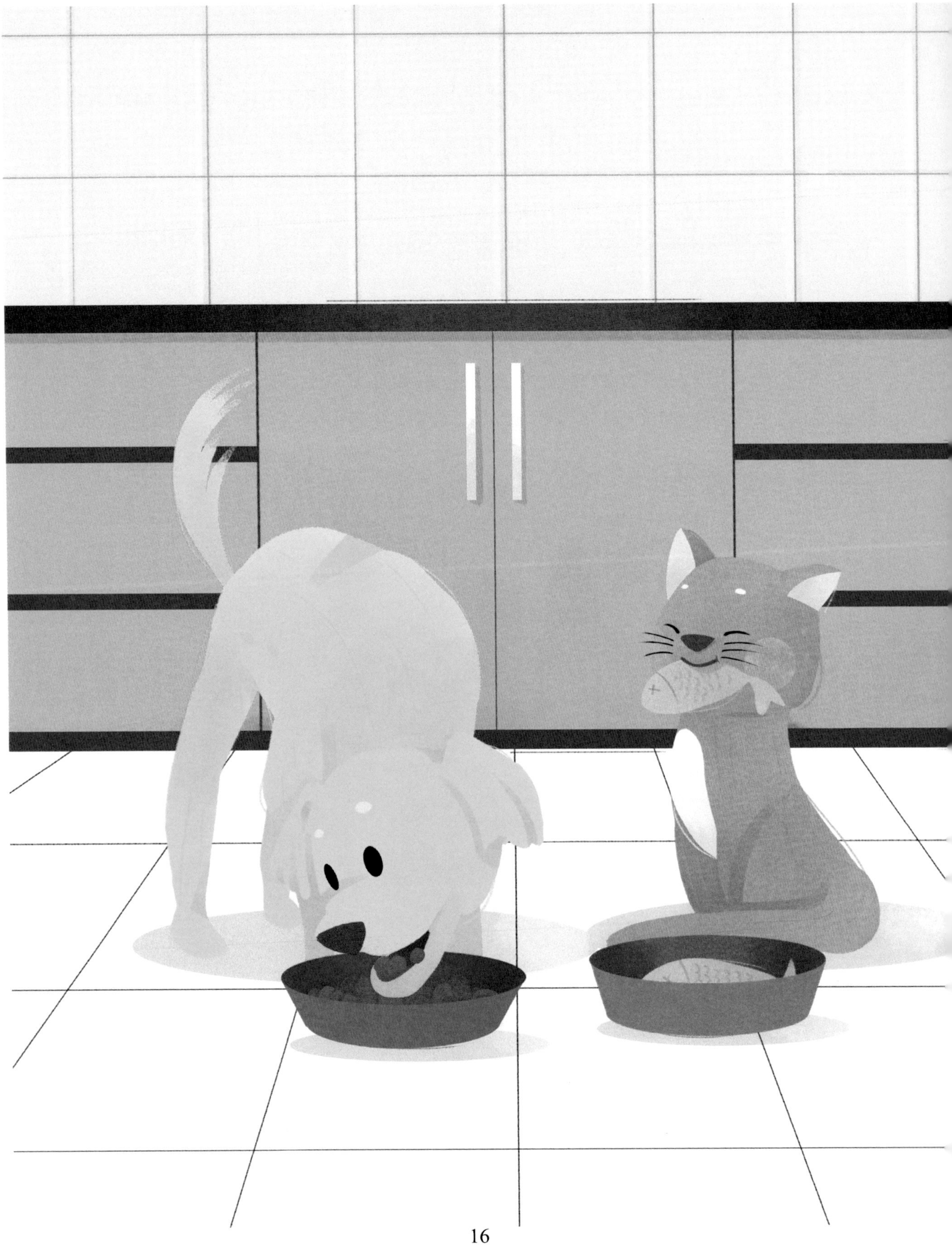

Sol stopped eating, wiped the kibble bits off his lips with his paw and said,

"I have never took the time to enjoy what I currently have, I think I will try that."

So he became mindful of the food he was eating with every bite, noticing every texture, and flavor.

He noticed his breathing became softer and calmer.

He suddenly felt immense appreciation for his owner for providing him with a delicious meal.

He smiled to himself.

When both Sol and Luna were done eating, they returned their bowls to the owner.

Sol barked and Luna meowed with deep appreciation.

The owner reached out to pet them and replied,

"I'm so glad you both enjoyed dinner!"

Sol turned to Luna and said,

"You know I never noticed how my owner pours the right amount of kibble in my bowl, until I took the time to focus on the food I was eating. She treats me with such kindness, I'm so grateful for that."

Luna replied,

"Staying in the present moment is such a wonderful gift, it allows you to realize how abundant your life is."

CHAPTER 3: LOVE FOR YOURSELF AND LOVE FOR OTHERS

Luna stayed the night after dinner.

Sol graciously made some room for Luna on his dog bed for her too, so they can both rest easy.

Everyone slept with the dull sound of rain gently tapping against the window.

The next morning, the light trickled softly into the window, grazing against Sol's face.

Sol noticed that it stopped raining and it was a bright, sunny morning.

Luna woke up too and turned to Sol,

"Look! The sun is always shining even behind the dark clouds."

Luna eventually moved from Sol's dog bed to a chair in the room.

Luna gently said,

"Every morning, I sit upright in a chair or comfortable position, close my eyes, and take some deep breaths in silence for a couple of minutes. It's called meditation."

Sol asked,

"Why do you start your day like that?"

Luna replied,

"It helps me stay and enjoy the present moment. It sets off my day with good intentions."

Sol smiled and asked Luna if he could join her.

Luna smiled back,

"Certainly."

After the meditation, Luna asked how Sol felt.

Sol gently replied,

"I feel calm and at ease, like a peaceful wave rushing over me. I'm ready to start my day with a clear mind."

Luna turned to Sol,

"Now that the weather is clear, I may leave and go back home now."

Sol felt a little sad and asked,

"Will you come visit again?"

Luna replied,

"Yes, I do not live too far from here. I'm glad to have you as a new friend."

Luna noticed that Sol was still a little sad and replied,

"Sol, something else I like to do is express love to myself and the people I care about. First, I say 'May I...' and follow it with some good intention. For example, I say 'May I give and receive appreciation today.' Then I think of a person I care about and say 'May you give and receive appreciation today.' Give it a try."

As Sol walked with Luna to the door, he felt compassion for their new friendship.

Luna waved goodbye and walked in the bright sunshine.

Sol closed his eyes and whispered to himself

"May I be happy. May I be safe. May I be healthy, peaceful and strong."

Then he shifted his attention to Luna and said

"May you be happy. May you be safe. May you be healthy, peaceful and strong."

ABOUT THE AUTHOR

Pearly Hidron is a passionate author exploring topics of growth, gratitude, and intentional living. She has a special interest in life-long learning and youth-related interests. She is a firm believer in the power of books to attain knowledge in living out a transformative life.

Her earliest memory was finding joy and solace reading a children's book in Pre-K.To recreate the same magic and comfort for all the young curious minds, this is her first book and she wrote it just for you.

Connect with Pearly here:
connectwithpearly@gmail.com

Made in the USA
Coppell, TX
09 July 2020

30412727R00019